Prince William

A Birthday Scrapbook

Prince William

A Birthday Scrapbook

by M. E. Crane

Aladdin Paperbacks
New York London Toronto Sydney Singapore

First Aladdin Paperbacks edition May 2000

Text copyright © 2000 by Simon & Schuster, Inc.

Aladdin Paperbacks
An imprint of Simon & Schuster Children's Publishing
1230 Avenue of the Americas
New York, NY 10020

Designed by Corinne Allen
The text of this book was set in Goudy.
Printed and bound in the United States of America
10 9 8 7 6 5 4 3 2

Library of Congress Catalog Card Number: 00-102028
ISBN 0-689-83532-9

Photograph copyright © 1999 AP/Worl Wide Photos

The Royal Birth
1982–1983

Photograph copyright © 1982 Snowdon/Camera Press London

Mum and Dad with the future king

In 1982, there were 626,000 children born in England and Wales. 321,000 of them were boys. In London, on June 21, 1982, four of those boys were born at St. Mary's Hospital, but only one would be the future king.

Michael Jackson releases *Thriller*, which sells more than 25 million copies, becoming the biggest-selling album in history

1982   1983   1984

1982–1983

William at his first photo session, age six months

William Arthur Philip Louis Windsor (whose real last name is Schlweswig-Holstein-Sonderborg-Glucksburg-Saxe-Coburg-Gotha) had a mother who was a princess and a father who is a prince. His great-great grandmother was Queen Victoria. His home was a palace. His playmates were dukes and duchesses. From the moment of his birth he was marked for greatness.

Chariots of Fire wins the Academy Award for Best Picture
The Vietnam Veterans Memorial is dedicated in Washington, D.C.

In some ways, William was like other children; he would be bathed and fed and clothed by his parents (in a break from royal tradition, Charles and Diana took care of little William themselves, instead of hiring a nanny.) But William was not like other children in one important way: His parents knew what he would be when he grew up—they **really** knew. Wills would not be a fireman or an airplane pilot or even a doctor or a lawyer. He would grow up to be the King of England.

Charles and Diana took William to Australia and New Zealand before his first birthday

Tokyo Disneyland opens

1984

Just before Wills turned two years old, another royal birth occurred. Prince Henry Charles Albert David—known to all as Prince Harry—was born on September 15, 1984, in the same hospital where William had been born. Though his mother was worried that the rambunctious William might be jealous of his new sibling, Wills took to Harry immediately. (Wills even got in trouble when he cried because he couldn't hold the new baby at Harry's christening.)

Photograph copyright © Snowdon/Camera Press Londo

Wills with his new brother, Prince Harr

Kathy Sullivan becomes the first U.S. woman to walk in space
The Coca-Cola company introduces New Coke. It's a disaster.

Because of their royal duties, Charles and Diana did need help with the two children. Barbara Barnes, a relaxed, fun, modern young woman, became their nanny. Even though Diana tried to keep their upbringing as carefree as possible, there was a lot of pressure from the Queen and the Queen Mother to keep the boys on a tight rope. Imagine having a queen as your grandmother! No wonder little Wills often acted up in the presence of his royal relatives!

William waves to the crowd

Photograph copyright © Retna Camera Press London

1986

1984–1985

Again breaking with tradition, Charles and Diana chose a nursery for William (most royal children were taught by governesses at home). When he was three years old, William was sent to Mrs. Mynor's Nursery School, just about one-half mile from his home, Kensington Palace. At first, the poor little guy didn't even know how to play with the other kids—he had never had friends his age!

Wills and mum take a stroll

William was happy in pre-school. He started in the Cygnets group, then moved to the Little Swans, and finally to the Big Swans. His favorite phrase was, "If you don't do what I want, I'll have you arrested!"

Wills's nickname was "Billy the Basher"

→ The charity rock concert, Live Aid, is held in London

1986

1986–1987

Prince William's fun-loving, irreverent style has always been part of his personality. When his uncle, Prince Andrew, was married to Sarah Ferguson in 1986, Wills was the only member of the wedding party who fidgeted, stuck out his tongue, and generally showed how boring the whole thing was to a four-year-old. While his jolly new aunt Sarah didn't mind, his stern father certainly did, and Wills's dear nanny was asked to leave. It was time for Wills to grow up.

Wills comes home after a day of classes

Photograph copyright © 1989 Glenn Harvey/Stills Retna Ltd

The Challenger disaster

1986

1987

Part of growing up was leaving Mrs. Mynor's safe haven and attending the Wetherby School, again very close to home. William adjusted to his new environment well. (His mother took him there by car every morning.) Diana was always home in the evenings to spend time with the boys. And on the weekends, William, Harry, and their parents would go to Highgrove House, their country home. One great thing about being a prince—there was always lots of space to run around, pets and ponies to play with and ride, and servants to clean up the mess. Nice!

The boys, looking spiffy in their school uniforms

U2's "With or Without You" becomes the number one song in the world

1988–1989

Prince William enjoying the English weather

By the time he was six, William was a very active boy. He loved sports of all kinds, especially when they involved going *fast*. He climbed fifty-foot trees and often had to be rescued by his bodyguards. Like his mother, he loved amusement parks, junk food, and change.

William and friends playing football

The Beatles are inducted into the Rock and Roll Hall of Fame
Tom Hanks plays a twelve-year-old in the movie *Big*

Wills playing a little one-on-one

Photograph copyright © 1987 Rex Features London

His father taught him to shoot. From age four, William loved to follow the men on their shooting courses, hunting for pheasants. By the time he was seven, Wills himself was handy with a hunting rifle.

William was also something of a ladies' boy, even as a child. He had gotten into the questionable habit of pinching the behinds of his friends' mothers. And even liberal Princess Diana thought he'd better stop that.

1990–1991

When you are a prince, and your mother and father may one day be king and queen, it might seem like everything in your future is rosy. But by the time William was eight years old, his family was starting to fall apart. And when your mom and dad stop talking to one another, it hurts a royal heart as much as it does a regular one.

The prince in a quiet moment

Home Alone becomes a box-office hit
Hubble Space Telescope is launched

1990

1991

The boys out for a ride

By 1990, Charles and Diana were leading very separate lives. They almost never appeared together in public, and when they did, they wouldn't look one another in the eye. The newspapers and television reports had nothing good to say about the state of their marriage. William's family was unraveling, and all he could do was watch.

1990–1991

Things got even tougher for William just before his ninth birthday. Quite by accident, a school friend struck William in the head with a golf club. The injury was severe, and Wills had to be rushed to the hospital (though his parents couldn't even agree on *which* hospital to send him to). He had suffered a fractured skull and he would require an extensive operation to keep the injury from becoming any graver.

*A royal splash,
Wills braves
the cold water*

Persian Gulf conflict begins in the Middle East

The operation was a success and the prognosis was a full recovery. He still has the scars.

Wills spent the rest of the year on his summer vacation and then went back to school in the fall. He was more active in sports than ever, and

William on a water park ride

he tried to concentrate on school work. He grew out of his little boy looks and began to look more and more like his glamourous mother.

1992–1993

Life gets complicated, even for princes

Imagine your parents are splitting up. Imagine everyone at school knows, and everyone at church, and all your friends' parents, even everyone in town. That's what most people have to deal with when their mom and dad get divorced. But if you're William Arthur

Barry Bonds named MVP by baseball's National League

Philip Louis Windsor, your mom comes to your boarding school to give you the news, and the next day the prime minister of the country announces it to the entire world.

This was not a great time for William. But true to form, he didn't fall apart when Diana told him there'd be a divorce. Like everyone else, he had seen it coming for a long time. In fact, he said to his mother, "I hope you will both be happier now."

Bill Clinton is inaugurated as president of the United States

1994–1995

When William turned thirteen he began attending a new school: Eton College. Eton was just a little more than five hundred years old when William arrived there. It was founded by one of his remote ancestors, Henry VI, in 1440. There are about one thousand boys there (no girls!), and all of them come from England's oldest (or wealthiest) families. Eton is situated in the town of Windsor. Wills was certainly the only kid whose grandmother owned the town fortress, Windsor Castle. Though William was probably the most famous Etonian, there were other boys who had bodyguards, complicated home lives, and newsworthy parents. Eton provided William with some of his closest friends.

Wills in his school uniform

South Africa has its first black president, Nelson Mandela
Wayne Gretzky is the highest scorer in the National Hockey League

A rugby moment:
Wills with his
Eton blokes

Like all the other Eton scholars, William wore the uniform proudly. The uniform was not the ordinary khaki pants and a white shirt. The Eton uniform is formal, with a white tie and a top hat and tails. When he went into town, William was pretty noticeable!

Eton's curriculum was traditional and tough. Wills studied English, chemistry, biology, physics, history, music, French, Latin, and Greek. He got up early, worked hard, and participated in sports such as rugby and crew. Eton was a haven for William during his teenage years. It was the one place William felt protected from the press and public of the outside world.

The prince declares victory

→ *Toy Story* opens

The prince flashes his winning smile

Charles and Diana were officially divorced in August, 1996, but for William, life went on. By now, Wills was a good-looking boy. He was over six feet tall with blonde hair, a great physique, and a gorgeous smile. He was as attracted to girls as they were to him. He spent hs winter breaks skiiing in Klosters and often dated the rich and famous. Klosters, Switzerland, is like Aspen, Colorado—lots of beautiful people in bright colors looking fabulous on the slopes. Wills, his mother, and his brother fit right in.

One-hundredth anniversary of Tootsie Rolls

William and
a friend hit
the slopes

1998

1996–1997

During this time, William was also introduced to a special friend of his mother's— Dodi Al Fayed. Dodi was the son of Mohamed Al Fayed, one of the richest men in the world. He enjoyed fast cars, speedboats, and huge mansions. It was a life Diana was attracted to, and when she asked her sons to join Dodi and her for a summer vacation in Saint-Tropez, France, it began to look like things were serious between Dodi and Diana.

The princes explore the great outdoors

Wills's last summer with his mum

Michael Jackson becomes a father

But the world would never know what might have been between them. Sometime after midnight on the night of August 31, 1997, a black Mercedes S-280, followed by dozens of press photographers, crashed in a tunnel in Paris. Only one man, Trevor Rees-Jones, survived—the one who was wearing a seatbelt. The other passengers died. They were the driver, Henri Paul; Dodi Al Fayed; and Diana, Princess of Wales.

It is not an exaggeration to say the whole world mourned Diana's death. But no one felt it more deeply than William and his brother Harry. Thousands of mourners left flowers outside of Buckingham and Kensington Palaces to commemorate their "Queen of Hearts." A state funeral was planned. Despite the divorce, Diana was eulogized and buried as a royal. William and Harry could not show the emotion they were feeling as they walked behind Diana's coffin with their father, grandfather, and uncle. Only the card on Diana's coffin on which Harry had written "Mummy" contained the enormity of their feelings.

Photograph copyright © Corbis

The royal family at Diana's funeral

→ Diana, Princess of Wales, is buried near her family home in Northamptonshire

1998–1999

—

Wills back into life again, sporting his Olympic jacket

If there is anything good that has come out of Diana's death, it is that Charles and his sons have become closer. Charles spent a great deal of time with William and Harry as

Titanic becomes the highest-grossing film of all time

they mourned the death of their mother. It was probably the only thing that kept them all going.

The prince's baby face

After the first year, William slowly emerged from his grieving and began to face life again. On March 3, 1998, William was ready for a public appearance. He embarked on a two-day tour of Canada . . . and the Canadians went wild. That is to say the Canadian *girls* went wild. William was a full-fledged heart-throb, dubbed "His Royal Sighness" by the press. South of the border, William caught on, too. His face appeared on teen magazines and he was named one of *People* magazine's 50 Most Beautiful People of 1998. Wills was enjoying his teen years, and the world was enjoying William.

Stock market goes wild because of Internet trading
John F. Kennedy, Jr. and his wife Carolyn Bessette die in a plane crash

The prince is almost legal!

The Present

As Prince William approaches his eighteenth birthday, the eyes of the world are on him. At the beginning of the year, the press reported that Wills "danced the night away" with a Norwegian friend, Anaaliese Asbjornsen, while on a skiing holiday. William is perhaps the world's most eligible bachelor, and on June 21, he's LEGAL!

Wills is doing what he can to reconcile his family, too. He took the bold step of visiting Sarah, Duchess of York, formerly the wife of his Uncle Andrew and a very close friend of Diana's, even though his family was not speaking to her. In the future, it's certain that this future king—who's always had a mind of his own—will continue to follow his heart.

What else does the future hold for William? There will certainly be romance, adventure, duty, and perhaps another royal bride. Prince William has lived through his first eighteen years with the grace and style that is his birthright. There's no doubt that this future king will display the same charisma, character, warmth, and style that has already charmed the world.

Y2K goes off without a hitch

2000

2001